nickelodeon™

TEENAGE MUTANT NINJA TURTLES™

GREEN MEANS GO!
FLASHLIGHT PROJECTOR

written by Michael Teitelbaum

studio fun BOOKS

White Plains, New York • Montréal, Québec • Bath, United Kingdom

THE GAUNTLET

April O'Neil, the Teenage Mutant Ninja Turtles' good friend and confidant, was walking down the street one day when suddenly she **(1)** found herself being chased by a giant pigeon.

She raced to the Turtles' secret underground lair.

"Guys! You'll never believe what happened to me," April said. "I'm being hunted by a **(2)** giant pigeon!"

"We're going to set a trap," said Leonardo.

"I know what we can use for bait," said Donatello.

"Bread crumbs?" suggested Michelangelo.

"I meant April," said Donatello.

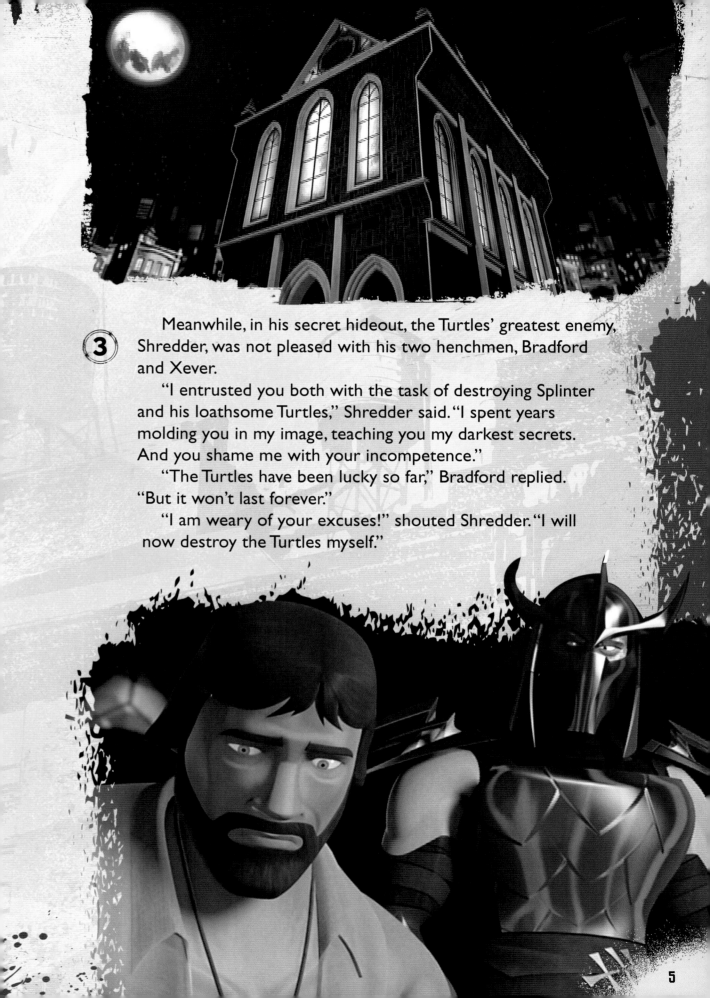

3 Meanwhile, in his secret hideout, the Turtles' greatest enemy, Shredder, was not pleased with his two henchmen, Bradford and Xever.

"I entrusted you both with the task of destroying Splinter and his loathsome Turtles," Shredder said. "I spent years molding you in my image, teaching you my darkest secrets. And you shame me with your incompetence."

"The Turtles have been lucky so far," Bradford replied. "But it won't last forever."

"I am weary of your excuses!" shouted Shredder. "I will now destroy the Turtles myself."

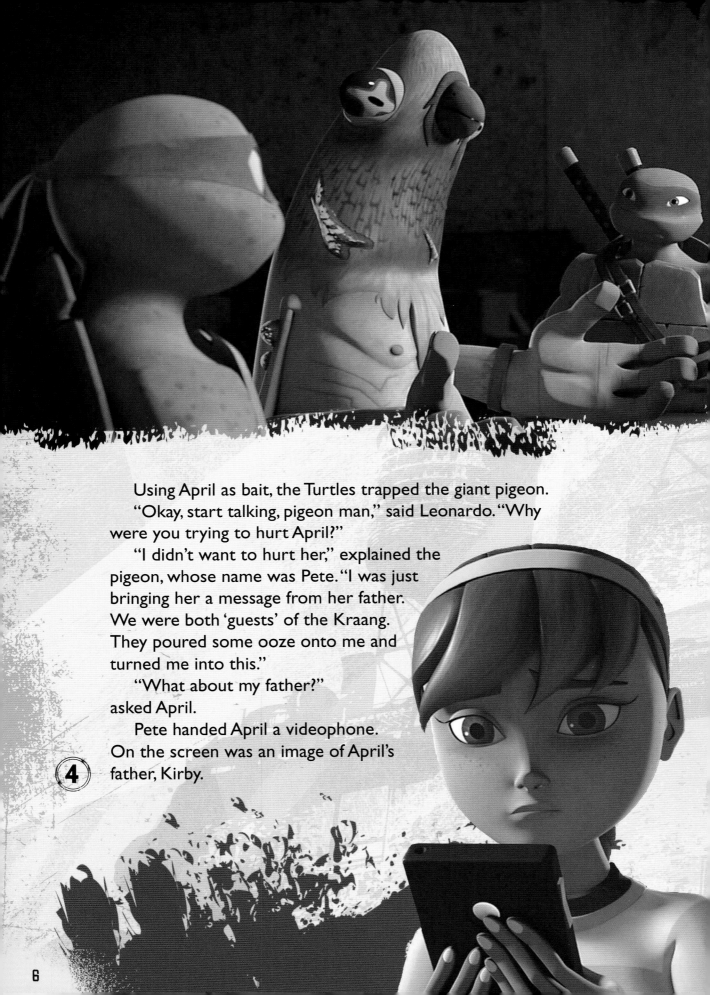

Using April as bait, the Turtles trapped the giant pigeon.

"Okay, start talking, pigeon man," said Leonardo. "Why were you trying to hurt April?"

"I didn't want to hurt her," explained the pigeon, whose name was Pete. "I was just bringing her a message from her father. We were both 'guests' of the Kraang. They poured some ooze onto me and turned me into this."

"What about my father?" asked April.

Pete handed April a videophone. On the screen was an image of April's father, Kirby.

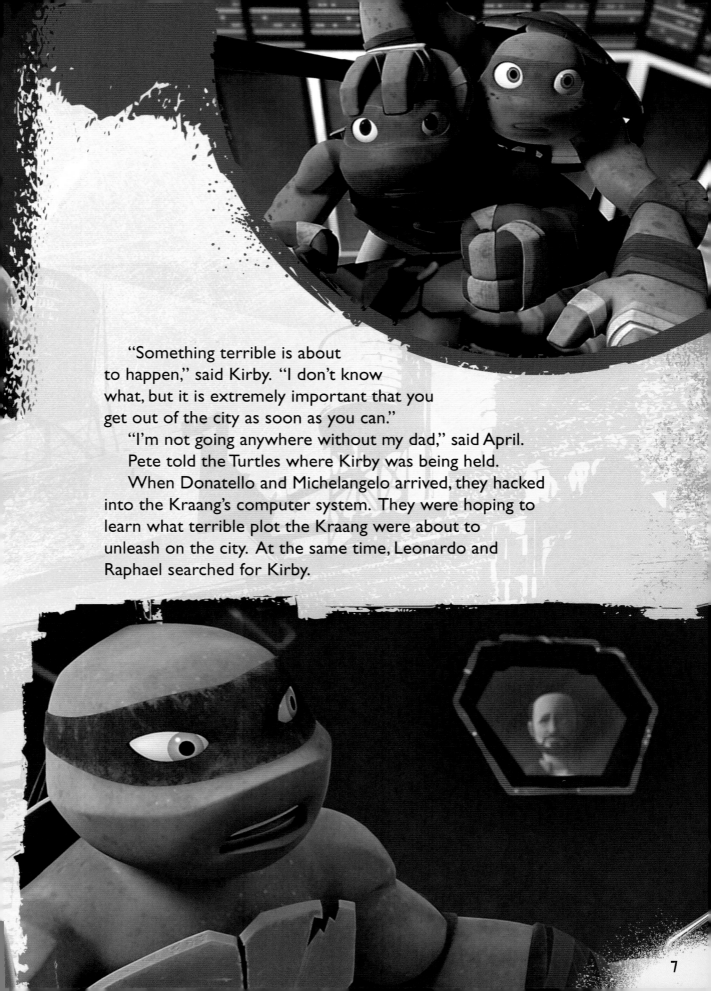

"Something terrible is about
to happen," said Kirby. "I don't know
what, but it is extremely important that you
get out of the city as soon as you can."

"I'm not going anywhere without my dad," said April.

Pete told the Turtles where Kirby was being held.

When Donatello and Michelangelo arrived, they hacked
into the Kraang's computer system. They were hoping to
learn what terrible plot the Kraang were about to
unleash on the city. At the same time, Leonardo and
Raphael searched for Kirby.

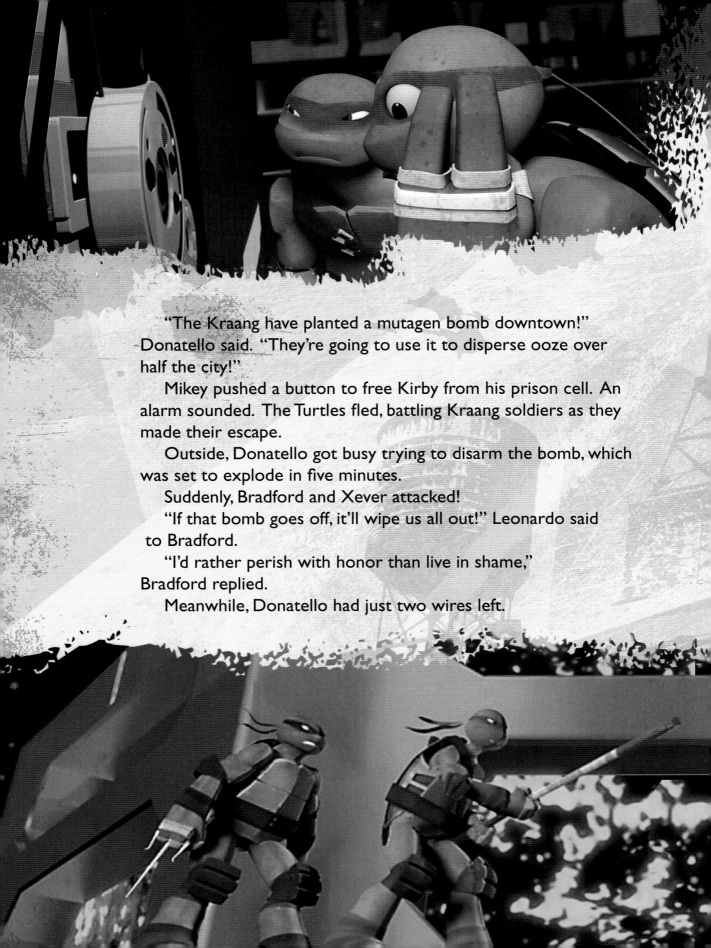

"The Kraang have planted a mutagen bomb downtown!" Donatello said. "They're going to use it to disperse ooze over half the city!"

Mikey pushed a button to free Kirby from his prison cell. An alarm sounded. The Turtles fled, battling Kraang soldiers as they made their escape.

Outside, Donatello got busy trying to disarm the bomb, which was set to explode in five minutes.

Suddenly, Bradford and Xever attacked!

"If that bomb goes off, it'll wipe us all out!" Leonardo said to Bradford.

"I'd rather perish with honor than live in shame," Bradford replied.

Meanwhile, Donatello had just two wires left.

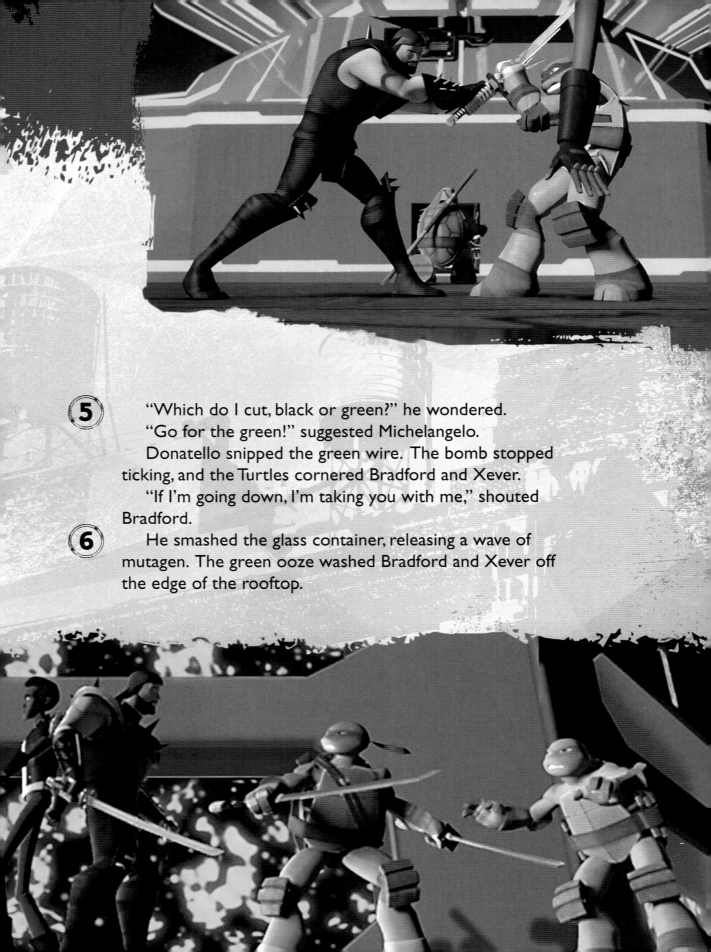

5 "Which do I cut, black or green?" he wondered.

"Go for the green!" suggested Michelangelo.

Donatello snipped the green wire. The bomb stopped ticking, and the Turtles cornered Bradford and Xever.

"If I'm going down, I'm taking you with me," shouted Bradford.

6 He smashed the glass container, releasing a wave of mutagen. The green ooze washed Bradford and Xever off the edge of the rooftop.

"So, to sum up," Leonardo began, "we kicked the butts of the Kraang and Shredder's top henchmen, while defusing a bomb and saving the city."

"Your skills are impressive," said a voice from above the Turtles. "But they will not save you!"

Shredder had shown up to finish off the Turtles himself. The Turtles tried their best to battle Shredder, but they were no match for his skills and power.

Shredder pinned Leonardo against a wall.

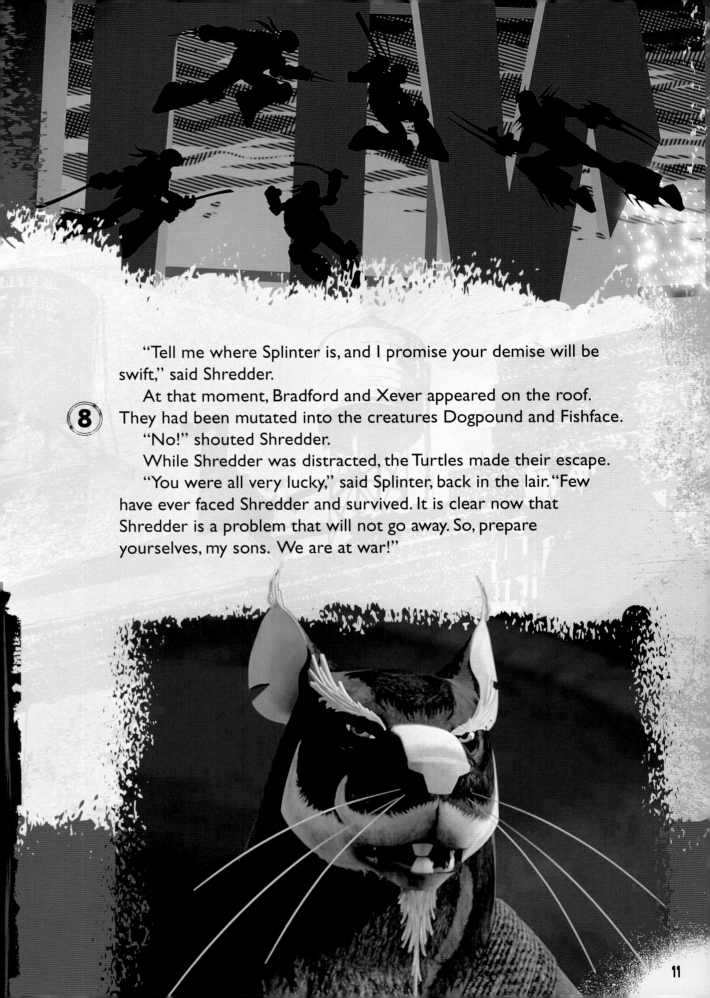

"Tell me where Splinter is, and I promise your demise will be swift," said Shredder.

At that moment, Bradford and Xever appeared on the roof. **8** They had been mutated into the creatures Dogpound and Fishface.

"No!" shouted Shredder.

While Shredder was distracted, the Turtles made their escape.

"You were all very lucky," said Splinter, back in the lair. "Few have ever faced Shredder and survived. It is clear now that Shredder is a problem that will not go away. So, prepare yourselves, my sons. We are at war!"

PANIC IN THE SEWERS

Splinter was worried. He knew that the time would come when the Turtles would have to face Shredder again. He also knew that they were not ready for that challenge.

"The last time you fought Shredder, you barely escaped with your lives!" Splinter said to the Turtles.

"But, Sensei, next time we'll be ready," said Raphael.

"Yes, because you will stay down here until you are ready," said Splinter forcefully. "No games. No rest. There is only training. Starting now."

Over the next few weeks, Splinter put the Turtles through a rigorous training regimen. The four brothers were exhausted.

"Sensei, we've been training nonstop for weeks!" Leonardo finally pointed out.

"Perhaps a brief rest is in order," said Splinter.

The Turtles really enjoyed their much-needed

2 break. Leonardo and Raphael watched TV, Michelangelo threw water balloons at his brothers, and Donatello worked on his all-

3 terrain patrol buggy.

While the Turtles were resting, April was on a mission of her own. Pretending to be a pizza deliverer, she brought a pizza to Sid and Fong, two of Shredder's henchmen.

Unknown to the henchmen, April had secretly attached a cell phone to the bottom of the pizza box. She returned to the Turtles' lair and used her own cell phone to help the Turtles listen in on the henchmen's plans.

4
5

"Shredder's got a plan to destroy the Turtles," said Fong. "He says they're in the sewers somewhere, and that's all he needs to know to wipe them out."

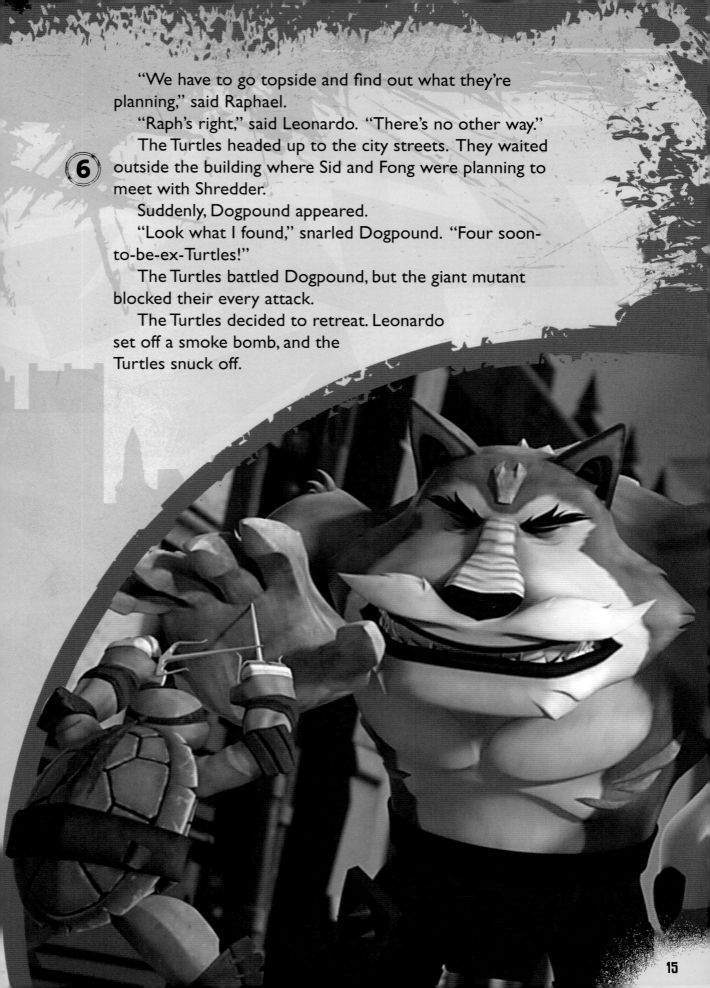

"We have to go topside and find out what they're planning," said Raphael.

"Raph's right," said Leonardo. "There's no other way."

The Turtles headed up to the city streets. They waited outside the building where Sid and Fong were planning to meet with Shredder.

Suddenly, Dogpound appeared.

"Look what I found," snarled Dogpound. "Four soon-to-be-ex-Turtles!"

The Turtles battled Dogpound, but the giant mutant blocked their every attack.

The Turtles decided to retreat. Leonardo set off a smoke bomb, and the Turtles snuck off.

6

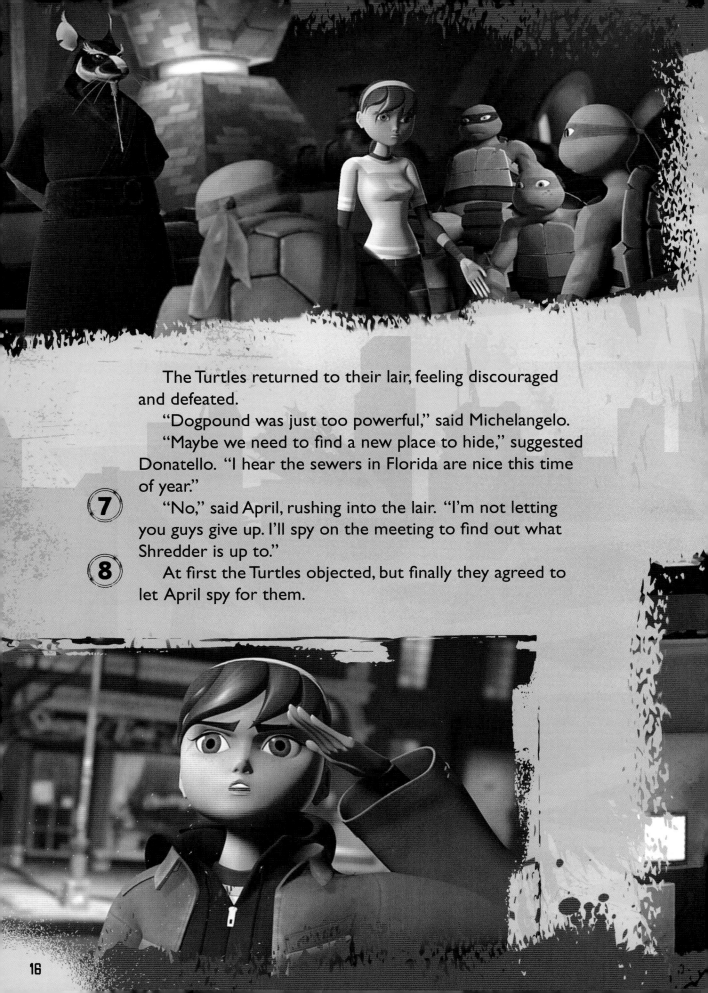

The Turtles returned to their lair, feeling discouraged and defeated.

"Dogpound was just too powerful," said Michelangelo.

"Maybe we need to find a new place to hide," suggested Donatello. "I hear the sewers in Florida are nice this time of year."

7   "No," said April, rushing into the lair. "I'm not letting you guys give up. I'll spy on the meeting to find out what Shredder is up to."

8   At first the Turtles objected, but finally they agreed to let April spy for them.

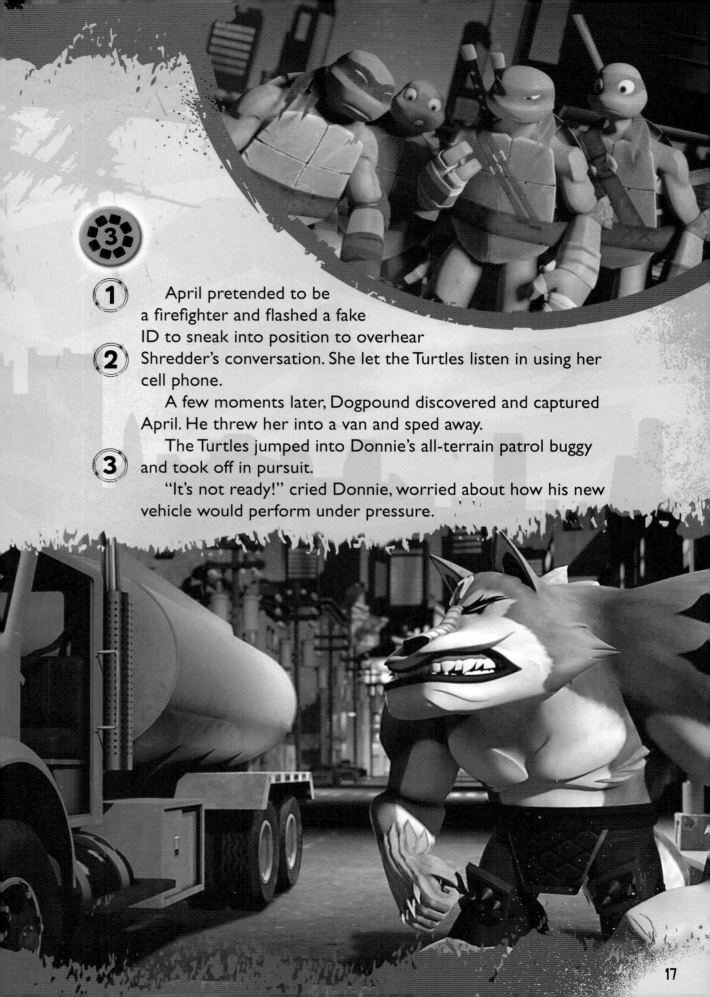

3

1 April pretended to be a firefighter and flashed a fake ID to sneak into position to overhear

2 Shredder's conversation. She let the Turtles listen in using her cell phone.

A few moments later, Dogpound discovered and captured April. He threw her into a van and sped away.

The Turtles jumped into Donnie's all-terrain patrol buggy

3 and took off in pursuit.

"It's not ready!" cried Donnie, worried about how his new vehicle would perform under pressure.

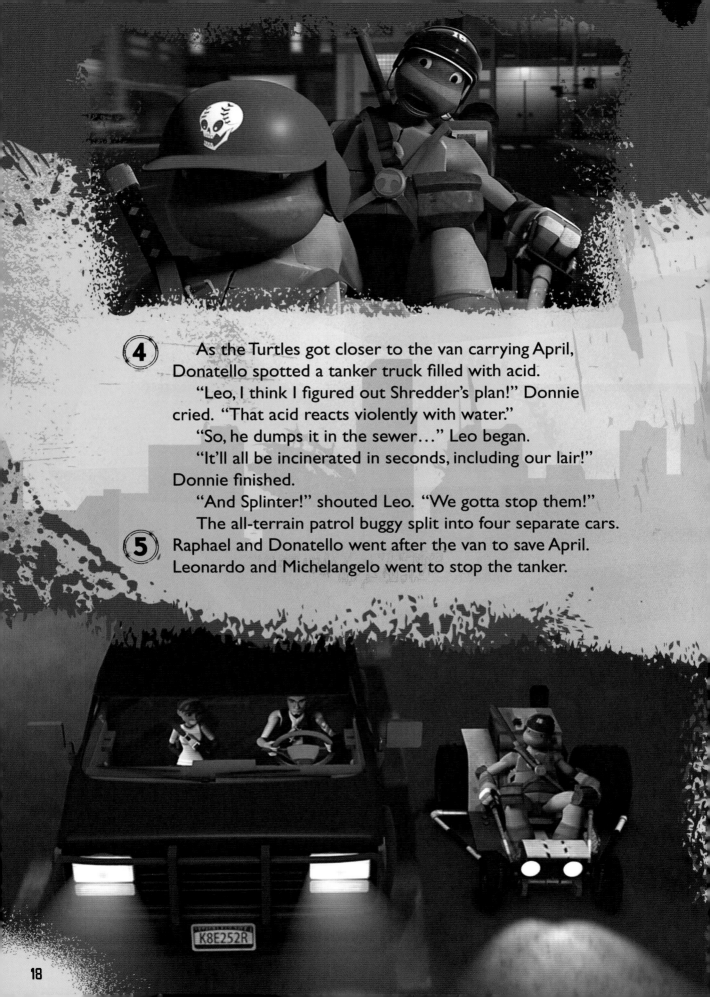

4   As the Turtles got closer to the van carrying April, Donatello spotted a tanker truck filled with acid.

"Leo, I think I figured out Shredder's plan!" Donnie cried. "That acid reacts violently with water."

"So, he dumps it in the sewer…" Leo began.

"It'll all be incinerated in seconds, including our lair!" Donnie finished.

"And Splinter!" shouted Leo. "We gotta stop them!"

5   The all-terrain patrol buggy split into four separate cars. Raphael and Donatello went after the van to save April. Leonardo and Michelangelo went to stop the tanker.

But first they had to get past Dogpound!
    While battling Dogpound, Leo accidentally

6 sliced open the tanker with his sword.
As acid poured from the tanker, Mikey
tossed a water balloon at it.

7   KA-BOOM!!
    The tanker exploded.
    Success! And Raphael and Donatello
had rescued April, too!

The Turtles had defeated Shredder's evil plan.

In his headquarters, Shredder was furious with Dogpound.

"They defeated you with go-karts and a water balloon!" he ranted.

"It won't happen again, Master. I promise you," said Dogpound.

"If you break that promise…" Shredder's words hung heavily in the air.

8 Meanwhile, back in their lair, the Turtles munched on a pizza to celebrate. Splinter spoke to his sons.

"I owe you my gratitude and an apology," he began. "It was not Shredder who fueled your fear, but me. You overcame that fear and performed admirably. No training today!"

The Turtles all cheered.

THE ALIEN AGENDA

On the rooftops of New York City, the Turtles battled an army of Kraangdroids. The Kraangdroids were robots operated by the Kraang aliens, who had no bodies of their own.

As he fought, Leonardo noticed Karai, one of Shredder's ninjas, observing from a nearby roof. He said nothing to his brothers as he took over the fight.

"I'll save you, Raph!" shouted Leo, jumping in front of his brother to defeat a Kraangdroid.

Later, back in their lair, Raph confronted Leo. He knew that Leo had been showing off to impress Karai.

"You knew Karai was watching!" he shouted and grabbed his brother in a headlock. Splinter broke up their fight.

"Your mission is to destroy the Kraangdroids and find Shredder," said Splinter. "Everything else is a distraction!"

Little did they know, at that moment Karai was back reporting to Shredder that she had seen the Turtles battling robots.

Earlier that week, April had sent a sample of her DNA to the Worldwide Genome Project, thinking it was part of a school assignment.

When she arrived at her school, it was deserted, but a woman was there waiting for her.

"Hello, I'm Ms. Campbell from the Worldwide Genome Project," said the woman. "Are you April O'Neil?"

"Um, yes," April replied.

"I'm here to present your DNA test results; come with me," said Ms. Campbell.

April grew suspicious. There was something about this that was just not right.

"I gotta go," said April.

2 But when she turned to leave, Ms. Campbell grabbed her arm.

April got free and ran through the school with Ms. Campbell chasing her. Hiding in a storage room, April sent a text message to the Turtles, who showed up to rescue her.

3 Ms. Campbell turned out to be a robot sent by the Kraang. The Turtles defeated her and rescued April.

The Turtles hurried to the Worldwide Genome Project.

"It looks like they're collecting DNA from every plant and animal species on Earth," said Donnie.

(4) Suddenly, Leonardo realized that Karai was there watching them.

(5) "Bet you think you're pretty slick," said Raph, attacking Karai.

"I have my moments," said Karai, battling back.

Leonardo tried to break up the fight, but he accidentally set off an alarm. An army of Kraangdroids marched into the room and joined the battle.

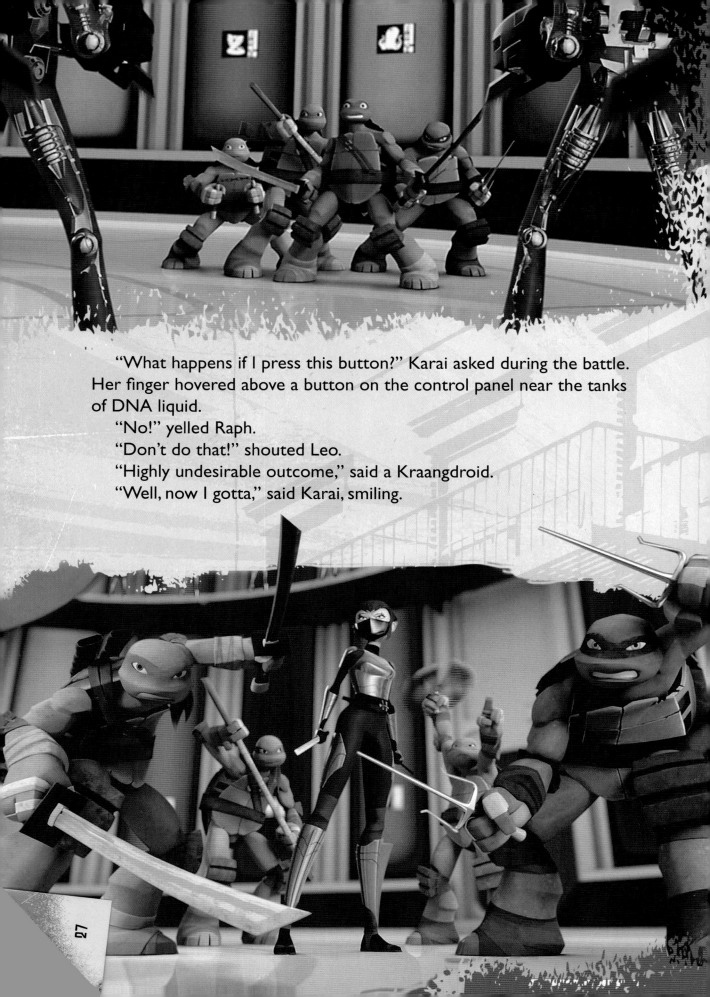

"What happens if I press this button?" Karai asked during the battle. Her finger hovered above a button on the control panel near the tanks of DNA liquid.

"No!" yelled Raph.

"Don't do that!" shouted Leo.

"Highly undesirable outcome," said a Kraangdroid.

"Well, now I gotta," said Karai, smiling.

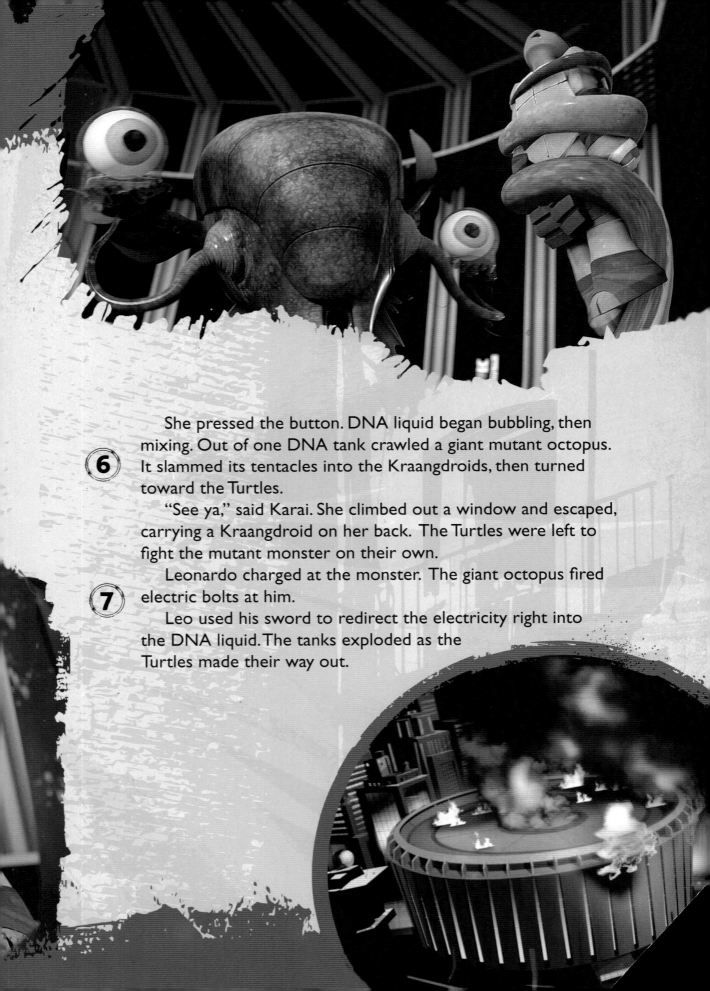

She pressed the button. DNA liquid began bubbling, then mixing. Out of one DNA tank crawled a giant mutant octopus. It slammed its tentacles into the Kraangdroids, then turned toward the Turtles.

6

"See ya," said Karai. She climbed out a window and escaped, carrying a Kraangdroid on her back. The Turtles were left to fight the mutant monster on their own.

Leonardo charged at the monster. The giant octopus fired electric bolts at him.

7

Leo used his sword to redirect the electricity right into the DNA liquid. The tanks exploded as the Turtles made their way out.

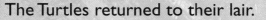

The Turtles returned to their lair.

"I'm sorry I didn't tell you all about Karai before," said Leo.

"You are not the first young man—or turtle—to make a fool of yourself over a girl," said Splinter. "However, when that girl is a deadly ninja in the employ of your enemy, that is an error you cannot afford. You must learn from your mistake."

8

"I know that now, Sensei," said Leonardo. "It will not happen again."